FiTTiNG OUT

The Friendship Experiment

HOW I MADE THREE NEW FRIENDS JUST IN
TIME FOR THE FIRST DAY OF SCHOOL!

By Sarah Giles

Birch Books

For Dad.

First Edition 2019

ISBN 978-1-948889-00-1

Birch Books Publishing — Washington, USA

COMPOSITION TITLE:

The Friendship Experiment

THIS NOTEBOOK BELONGS TO:

Max McConk

Contents

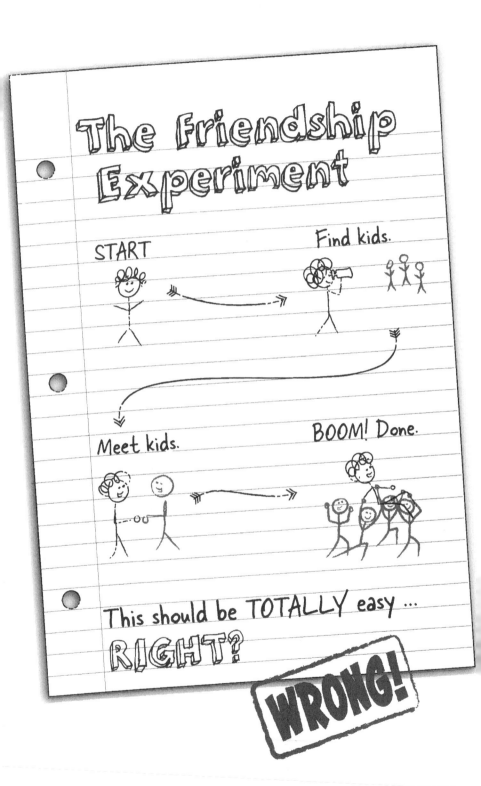

Introduction

Hiya! I'm Max. This is so exciting—
you are holding in your hands
the official scientific notebook for
my recent friendship experiment!
Because of this experiment, I went
from being a solo act, party of one,
Max McLonely, to a guy who knows
the secret to being able to find
friends anywhere!

As you read through my
experiment, you will find out more
about me too. For example, I can
be kind of a know-it-all, but not
because I want to prove how smart
I am. It's just that whenever I learn

something new, I just can't wait to tell someone about it! Besides, what else would I talk about?

I actually don't mind being called a nerd. I think that one day nerds will rule the world. *If you think about it, it's already starting to happen!*

My brother calls me a bona fide N-E-R-D. The funny part about that is that I don't even think he knows what "bona fide" means. (To be honest, I had to look it up too.) It means "real, true, or actual".

So, while we are on that subject ... if I use words that YOU don't know, there are two things

you can do: First, there is a glossary in the back of this book with some weird or tricky words and their meanings.

Second, as you are reading, you will see this foot picture: 👣. That's a signal to head to the bottom of the page for more information. This is called a "footnote." Get it? Foot-note!

Now on to the friendship experiment!

Footnote – Information that is placed at the bottom of the page to give additional explanation without interrupting the flow or rhythm of the text above.

CHAPTER 1: DAY ZERO

UGH! This can't be happening! Miguel, my best friend for pretty much my entire life, just moved away! Miguel is my Sure, I have a real *brother* at home, but that's not the same. BROs are forever!

Mom always says that Miguel and I are like two peas in a pod, but I like to say we are as tight as last summer's T-shirts.

Since I was three years old, it was Miguel and me against the world. Well, not really *against* it; maybe just him and me *in* the world. Anyway, it was always him and me. Now it's just me.

Miguel is now living in a town more than three hours away. I used to be able to ride my bike to his house in under ten minutes. To get to his *new* house, I would need to ride my bike, two city buses, and a ferryboat (and Dad won't let me go by myself).

So now who will I  out with every day? Who will laugh at my hilarious but sometimes weird jokes? Miguel seems to be the only person who realizes how funny I am. When will I get to talk to him again?

I guess we will just have to figure out how to be long-distance friends FOREVER.

THIS IS US 75 YEARS FROM NOW ... STILL BROS.

Bump!

But while he is gone, I still want someone to build forts with, play speed chess with, and sit with during lunch period. School starts in just one month, and without Miguel there, I'll be totally alone! It seems that I'll have to …

… make some new friends, and I only have a month to do it!

The last seventeen times that I made a new friend, Miguel was standing right by my side, AND he did all of the talking. The time before that was when I met Miguel,

and he did all of the talking that time too.

I met Miguel in preschool. In our classroom, the cubbies were arranged in alphabetical order. Miguel's cubby was right next to mine, since we are both M's.

On Monday, Miguel said, "Hi!" I just stared at him. On Tuesday, Miguel said, "Hi, Max!" I smiled nervously and ran over to the train table. On Wednesday, Miguel said, "Hey, cool ninja shirt!" I looked down at my shirt, looked back up at Miguel, and just nodded my head in agreement.

On Thursday, Miguel pointed

to my lunchbox and asked, "Hey, buddy, what's for snack today?" (His dad told him that if he asked me a question, he would be able to get me talking.)

I very quietly answered, "Um, artichokes" and I opened my bear-shaped container to show him.

Miguel's eyes opened wide. "Arti-WHAT? AAH! WHAT THE HECK IS THAT?" We both started laughing, and the rest is history.

So you

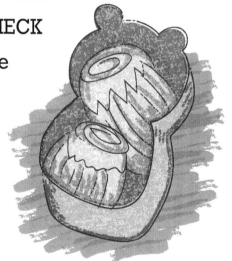

see, I am not totally shy all of the time, just at first. Once I know you, I will talk, sing, tell you about all five stages of the life cycle of a star, but it takes me a while to warm up to *new* folks.

Blech! Just thinking about having to make new friends makes my hands sweaty (which won't make the whole thing any easier).

Mom says, "C'mon, Max. Kids will love you. Just show them that winning smile!"

MY **SMILE** IS A WORK IN PROGRESS, BUT I *THINK* IT IS GETTING BETTER

Day 1

Preschool

1st Grade

Last Year

So, there are tons of kids all around where I live: there are kids in my neighborhood, at the park, at the pool ... everywhere. It seems like it should be easy to find kids to hang out with, but fitting in isn't easy for dudes like me.

I'm just ... different. You might be wondering, "How different could he *really* be?" Well, buckle up, Buttercup, you're about to find out! (See? Do you know anyone else who says stuff like that?)

OK. I think it's time to give you the full Max experience ...

CHAPTER 2:

Bio – Maximilian McConk

I'll start with the easy stuff: My full name is Maximilian Alexander McConk, and I am 10.85 years old. I have curly black hair. LOTS of curly black hair. I live in a blue house with my mom, dad, Pop-Pop, and my older brother.

What you must also know about me is that there are two hobbies that I love more than anything else. By

coincidence, they are the same two things that drive my big brother absolutely **NUTS**—hee hee.

First, I read a lot. I have read so many books that I have lost count. You name it, I have read about it. This means that I probably have close to a million random facts stored in my head. But it doesn't stop there: I love to talk about all the facts I pick up, especially the weird ones, like basically anything related to water bears.

Second, I love to find rhymes for words. I think this will make it much easier to live out my plan to become a chart-topping, album-dropping rap battle champion someday. (Either that or a doctor.) Anyway, when I have something really important to say, I figure it sounds better when I make it rhyme.

Now that you know a little more about how I roll, I am going to take it a step further and tell you EVERYTHING!

I have prepared the following official "bio" (short for "biography"), telling you all about what it means to

be me. (And it rhymes, of course.)

This Way to
Max's Bio

Official Bio

Maximilian McConk

My name's Maximilian,
    but I go by Max.
Ahead is a list of
    the MAX-i-est facts.

My bio contains all the things
    that are ME

And while in this list
    you might possibly see
one or two bits of YOU,
    you would have to agree
that all these together are

unique, LEVEL 3.

Not Your Everyday... Marches to Own Drummer... WHOA!

1 2 3

UNIQUE-O-METER

IN THE STANDARD INTERNATIONAL SCALE OF UNIQUENESS, **LEVEL 3** IS THE HIGHEST. (NOT MANY PEOPLE KNOW THAT.)

MAX FACTS

1. I wear Pop-Pop's racing goggles instead of a hat.

2. I've got a robot named Switches, a fish, and a cat.

SWITCHES

PROFESSOR PUFFYPANTS ("PEEPS" FOR SHORT)

3. Astronomy Club, now that is MY JAM!
No one is more into stars than I am.

4. I ride a sweet "UNI"
and know lots of tricks.

SWEET
UNICYCLE

5. I once built a YURT
out of popsicle sticks.

6. My favorite lunch is Dad's bouillabaisse stew.

7. I know more about TURTLES than most people do.

FOR EXAMPLE, I'LL BET YOU DIDN'T KNOW THAT NESTING FEMALE LEATHERBACK **TURTLES** MAKE NOISES THAT SOUND LIKE A HUMAN **BURP**.

8. I like to READ about music and sing about BOOKS.

9. My CAPE probably looks different than your CAPE looks ...

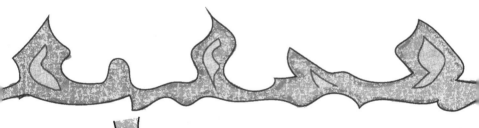

WAIT ... DO YOU NOT HAVE A **CAPE**? YOU SHOULD CONSIDER GETTING ONE. THEY PROVIDE BOTH STYLE AND **AERODYNAMICS!**

Footnote There is debate in the community of superhero experts as to whether a superhero's cape *actually* provides an aerodynamic advantage or is simply used to add mucho style.

Drraaagg!

(Continued) Though not believed to help much with flying, it is generally accepted that a cape would provide slight drag force.

10. I take BANJO lessons
each Friday at four.
(Most kids take guitar,
but I like banjo more.)

11. I'm MEGA-bad at football
and can't really dance.

ME

12. I once spent a whole weekend
RESEARCHING ants …

FOR FUN!

After reading through this list, you are probably thinking, "Whew! That's a lot of *different* packed all into one guy!". But this is the way I have always been: one in a million, unique level 3.

CHAPTER 3: The EXPERiMENT

Let's look at this like a math problem: Question #1 – Max has 1 best friend. 1 best friend moves away. How many best friends does Max have left? That's right, ZERO BEST FRIENDS!

Question #2 – In Max's neighborhood, there are 0 kids who look like Max, 0 kids who talk like Max, and 0 kids who have the same

hobbies as Max. How many kids in the neighborhood are like Max? NONE! ZERO KIDS are like Max!

Question #3 – Max is pretty shy. It often takes him 3 times of seeing someone before he feels brave enough to talk. How many kids has Max talked to when seeing them for the first time? ZERO! Max has talked to ZERO KIDS the first time he met them.

So, to sum it up:
Lonely + different + shy = YIKES!

I have a feeling that *wanting* friends ain't enough ... I don't think this is going to be as easy as Mom says it is. Most kids figure out how

to do this in kindergarten. I didn't
have to, because I had Miguel.
Now here I am, about to go into fifth
grade, and I have NO IDEA where
to start.

I wish there was a book about
how to do this. Like this book that
I got from the library that tells you
how to do 101 different science
experiments. It tells you exactly
what supplies you need, what to
do with them, and in what order. It
even has pictures showing you what
it should look like along the way.

Science I get. It just makes
sense to me. But people? I am totally
confused when it comes to what

makes people "tick." Science follows sets of rules. People are so ... random! Hmm, I think I know what I need to do ...

Do I need a magic spell? Or friend-sniffing GIANTS?

No ... To solve my friend
shortage, I think I'll use ...

SCIENCE!

SWITCHES,
to the
Max-CAVE!

SCIENTIFIC METHOD:

*Observe a problem to solve

*Ask questions → HOW do I
find some??

Need
friends!

*Form a hypothesis

*Test and record what happens

*Conclusion

To find some new friends, I will conduct a scientific friend-finding

So, according to the scientific method, the first step is to observe a problem. That's easy: I NEED to find some friends, PRONTO!

Step two, ask questions. How does it work? What do I say? What

do I do with my arms? What if my cheeks get so hot that my head explodes? "HOW IN THE WORLD AM I GOING TO DO THIS?"

CHAPTER 4:
Hypothesis #1 –
New ME?

Step three: form a hypothesis (an idea that I can prove by testing it). Hmm ... what is the secret to making friends?

Last summer, I read this book about animal friendships. I found out that cows actually have best friends—just like me and Miguel!

The book also said that baboons form friend groups by joining up with others who are just like them. This makes me think that making new friends might be all about FITTING IN.

Maybe I can fit in with the other kids by making a few little changes here and there. OK ... maybe big changes.

I could hide just a few of the things that make me me, and prove that I can be just like everyone else. The new me will blend in perfectly. I can't wait! This is gonna be AWESOME!

How have I not thought of this before? It seems so simple! I just need to figure out what *normal* kids

are like and be more like that. Once I have become just like them, they will have no choice but to be friends with me. If it works for baboons, it should work for me, right?

My new friends and I will only do cool things. No unusual things; definitely no WEIRD things. But … wait. Uh-oh … What are cool things? What aren't?

Maybe I could act more like my big brother, Matt. People seem to like him, and he has a LOT of friends, so he must be doing something right.

Matthew McConk
7th Grade

"Most likely to be most liked"

Have a great summer, man!

I♡U Matt!!   You ROCK!

So here it is, me as a cool tween sensation:

I'll abbreviate most words.
(It makes Mom CRAY CRAY.)

I'll have FOMO on YOLOs
and ACROs for DAYS!

"ACRO" IS AN **ABBREV** FOR "ACRONYM."
I JUST MADE IT UP BECAUSE I AM
NOW VERY **TRENDY**. BY THE TIME **YOU**
USE IT, IT WILL PROBS BE OVER...

I'll abbreviate evs,
    like any good TWEEN,
until even I am not sure what I mean!

GLOSSARY OF ABBREVs and ACROs

ABBREV (Abbreviation = Short form of a word.)

Cray cray = Crazy
Evs = Everything
Probs = Probably
'Stache = Mustache
'Do = Hairdo

ACRO (Acronym = A word formed by using only the first letter of each word in a phrase.)

FOMO = "Fear Of Missing Out"
YOLO = "You Only Live Once"

I will totally change
    how I talk to include
having whole conversations
    with just the word "dude."

OK, so if I pretend to be a lot more like Matt and a lot less like me, I could probably fit in with just

about anyone.

I have it all figured out! With science on my side, there's NO WAY this won't work!

CHAPTER 5: It Didn't Work!

MISTAKE #1: HAVEN'T GOTTEN THE HANG OF STYLING MY HAIR YET.

MISTAKE #2: MUSTACHE DRAWN ON UNTIL REAL ONE COMES IN. PROBABLY SHOULDN'T HAVE USED PERMANENT MARKER!

MISTAKE #3: BORROWED COLLARED SHIRT FROM MATT. IT'S A LITTLE ROOMY ...

CHAPTER 6:

Hypothesis #2 -

~~New ME?~~

NEW THEM?

So, that was clearly NOT the right
hypothesis. Oh, man, what
a disaster! That was the *opposite* of
what I wanted to happen. So maybe
I need to try to do the *opposite* of
that. What is the opposite of proving

that I can fit in with all the other kids? Aha! Maybe the other kids need to fit in with ME for this to work.

So ...

Why should I have to UNLIKE
what I like?
Who says that I must ride a
regular bike?

What some may call weird,
my mom calls "distinct."
And I am just
INTERESTING,
not weird at all! <wink>

Maybe I am the COOL one!
       Could this possibly be?
Would it be great if
       more kids were like ME?

Would we get along best
       if we always agree?

Hmm ... Ooh, next GREAT IDEA

       coming in

1 .. 2 .. 3 ...

Maybe I should find friends
       exactly like me,
who journal and banjo and
       practice Tai Chi.

46

Who love to snowshoe
    and to bowl and to 'cache
and have a respectable
    polished-rock stash.

THIS IS AN ABBREV FOR
"GEOCACHING." HMM...
MAYBE ABBREVS AREN'T
ACTUALLY THAT BAD...

Don't know this word?
Check the glossary!

I was thinking about what
this would be like as I fell asleep.
I had this wild dream, where I was
hanging out with, well ... ME. A
lot of MEs. Everywhere I looked,

it was just me. It was kind of like when you look in a mirror with a mirror behind you, and it seems like you see yourself over and over into infinity, but in my dream, all of the selves were just hanging around in my living room.

At first it was fun.

Footnote Spud is a super fun game. All you need is a ball and a few friends. Check the glossary for a full guide on how to play.

When I woke up, I realized
that only being with kids who
were just like me would be, well,
a nightmare. Mega-boring! How
would I ever learn anything new?

Nah—I don't even have to test
that hypothesis to know it won't
work. I wonder ...

Do the best friendships happen to be made with a little VAR-I-E-TY?

Variety is called "the spice of life," based on the idea that life is more interesting when you change things up.

CHAPTER 7: EUREKA!

Yeah, I think I may be on to something here ... Who cares if we don't like the same things? It actually doesn't matter so much.

Take the example of Switches and my goldfish, Finn. What could be more different than a fish and a robot? But they love to hang out together, and Switches says they actually have lots in common.

One is a robot and one is a fish, but *even they* sometimes wish the same wish ...

So I don't need to find someone just like me, or someone who likes everything I like. I won't *always* have to play what they like, and they don't *always* have to play

what I like. I just need to find kids who want to … play!

Maybe it's as simple as that!

I should just BE MYSELF and so should my friends.
Since all of us
ARE who we ARE,
in the end.

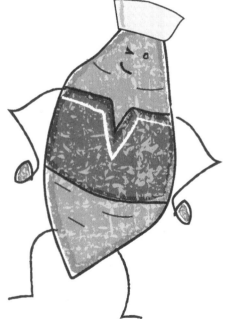

CHAPTER 8:
Hypothesis #3 -
~~NEW ME?~~ ~~NEW THEM?~~
JUST BE MAX!

Luckily, there is a big wide world full of nice kids, so I will just get back out there and try another hypothesis!

To recap the experiment so far: Hypothesis #1: try to become

a different kid; one who could fit in with everyone: FAIL. Hypothesis #2: try to find kids who are just like me: BORING.

The way I see it, there is only one other way to do this. I need to get out there, give 'em the full Max experience, and see if *that* is the secret to instant friendship.

Here's the plan:

1. Go where tons of kids are ... the park!

2. Walk up and ... eek ... talk to them.

3. Be the same guy I am, all day, every day.

So it seems like the best way
to meet a new bro
is just TRY, be LESS SHY*,
and just be MAX, ya know?

*BEING LESS SHY IS ABOUT AS EASY FOR ME AS BEING A PURPLE PLATYPUS... SO I AM TRYING A "FAKE IT TILL YOU MAKE IT" APPROACH.

'SUP

With steps 1–3, it should
    work out just fine.
I should find some dudes whose
    new-bro needs match mine.

But what if the real ME
    can't find any matches?
Sometimes YOU do YOU,
    but then no one attaches.

Mom said:
"Trust me, it'll happen;
    just try, try again.
Then one day … it works, and
    BOOM! You've got a friend!"

So I'll follow these steps
    to a T nonetheless,
and with luck, sometime soon,
    ADiOS, loneliness!

And having good friends,
    man oh man,
will be GREAT!

It might take a while,
    but is SOOOOOOO
worth the wait!

CHAPTER 9:
Test, Test, Test

Now any good plan may
        look just fine on paper,
but time to start testin'
        and launch a

FRIEND CAPER!

Pop-pop (remembering his

days as a paper salesman) told me

to start off with a joke. He said it's

much easier to get people to agree to what you want once you have them laughing.

I also think I should wear my favorite shirt and, of course, my goggles, but maybe not my cape. I have to leave some surprises for the first time we hang out!

Monday morning, after breakfast, I walked over to the park at the end of my street to see if I could wrangle some new bros. I saw some kids standing together at the edge of the playground. I was feeling totally ready, mega-brave, and extra Max-y, until they turned around and looked at me.

And then, I … forgot …
EVERYTHING! I just stood there,
trying to remember my plan; what
to say, what to do.

The whole time I felt like
my head might
explode. I
am pretty sure my
face was beet red.
Have you ever
seen a beet? It's
so red it's almost
purple, and so was
my face at that moment.

Ok, now! I shouted to myself
inside my head. *It doesn't matter
what you say anymore. Just say*

something ... ANYTHING!! NOW, Max! SPEAK!!

I swallowed a painful gulp and opened my mouth, but it was like my voice got stage fright, and nothing came but a sort of honk-squeak. Something like the sound a goose makes when it's really mad or sick.

The group of kids were frozen like statues. They just stood there, looking at me blankly, not sure what to say. And so what did the new and improved mega-brave Max do? I RAN! I ran far, far away ...

and FAST!

I ran all the way home and actually got there in less than three minutes. (I decided that I may add cross-country running to my list of hobbies because it seems that I'm pretty good at it.)

As I ran, I replayed those horrible embarrassing moments in my head. *Could it have really been as bad as I remember? Yeah ... it WAS that bad.*

I couldn't give up and let the experiment end this way. I HAD TO try again. I went into the kitchen to pour a big glass of chocolate almond milk and make plans for another hard day of field

experiments tomorrow.

Hypothesis #3, Day 2

C'mon, Max, you can do this.
Today is a great day for a do-over. I
gave myself a pretty solid pep talk
as I walked down the street, back
to the scene of yesterday's disaster:
the park. *This is it. You got this. It's*
showtime, Max!

I walked into the park, ready
to take a second crack at my
hypothesis. After all, being myself
should be the easiest thing I can be.
I don't even have to try to be me,

because I'm me!

I finally felt ready to try again.
Anyway, Mom said sometimes it
takes a couple of tries.

Try #2:

Not proud of this fact,
    but I'm not gonna lie:
the second try TANKED
    and I started to cry.

Nobody saw, but I felt like a BABY.
(But I think everyone cries
    sometimes, maybe?)

Try #3:

The THIRD time,
I took a deep breath,
jumped back in.

Bad timing. Struck out and

BLURGH!

I cried AGAIN.

Try #4:

The fourth time was sure to work out! (It did not.)

They stared as if I had EIGHT heads. (I do not.)

I was starting to wonder if this experiment was ever going to work. Was I doomed to walk this earth alone? Sitting at the end of the lunch table by myself, having pretend phone conversations with my imaginary friends on an unpeeled banana? NO! I couldn't let that happen. Not without a fight!

I decided it had been a long-enough morning of trying to make friends. After all, the only thing that I had actually done was freak out a large number of local kids, who, by the way, had begun standing around in clusters, pointing at me and sharing stories

about their encounter with "that weird boy over there." One girl called me "that *nice* boy over there," so I guess I could consider that a small victory.

It seems that all of my attempts to meet new kids has brought *them* together as new friends, but without *me*. I decided to call it quits and head home, (running, of course).

CHAPTER 10: Bzzzz!

When I got to my door, Mom shouted from the kitchen. "Max, is that you? How did it go, honey?" She came into the hallway and saw the defeated look on my face.

After staring at me for a minute as if she was trying to figure something out, she said, "Wait right there. I think I know something that can help."

She left for a few minutes and
then came back and handed me
a rolled-up piece of paper and an
oatmeal cookie. (I do find it helpful
when important papers have
cookies attached to them.)

I had a feeling that this paper
was going to be another one of
Mom's wacky stories. Her stories
always seem at first like they are just
a bunch of strange ideas that aren't
leading to anything. They are a little
hard to follow, but they always end
with exactly what we need to know
in order to solve our problems.

(We found out that most of
her stories actually come from old

rock music videos that she watched when she was in college.)

She loves to come up with rhymes too. Where do you think I learned it? Well, actually, it was partly from Mom and partly from the tooth fairy, who is also very good at rhyming.

Anyway, I unrolled the paper Mom gave me, took a bite of the cookie, and began reading:

From the desk of MELINDA McCONK

MOM

There's this band playing music
    in a field full of flowers.
Then a girl in a bee costume
    tap-dances for hours.

She taps, shuffles, and twirls
    for each person she meets,
But they don't get the bee thing,
    so she wanders the streets.

The dancing bee feels sad
    until she looks up and sees
A garden that's swirling
    with what? DANCING BEES!!

Folks dressed in gold tutus
    and bicycle pants,
They welcome her in,
    and together they dance.

The sad bee is now happy
    to finally be
In a place where it's cool
    to just be her own bee.

"Thanks, Mom. That was a really weird story. What does it have to do with me?"

She said, "It's simple really: you just need to find YOUR bees! If kids don't get the whole 'Max thing,' then they may not be the kids you are looking for. You've just got to keep looking. I know this isn't easy, but, sweet boy, please don't quit!"

But I really, really, really wanted to quit, to give up, maybe even move away. After one LAST try.

Official Field Guide to Finding YOUR Bees:

"Your cape is weird ... I love it!"

Maybe your bee!

"Your cape is weird ... I hate it!"

Probably not your bee ...

"Your cape is weird ... I hate YOU!"

Aaaah!! Definitely NOT your bee! RUN AWAY!!!

"Did you make THAT thing?"
Probably not your bee.

"Did you make that thing?"
Maybe your bee ...

"Did you make that thing?
Aw, cool!   Now check out
THIS thing that I made!"
Bzzzz! Definite bee potential!

CHAPTER II: SUCCESS!

Then, out of the blue, on the fifth try—

KaPOW!

Something just *clicked* and I've got a friend now!

OK, OK, you are probably wondering how this happened. So let me back up a step. I can't explain *why* it worked, but I'll tell you *how*. It started out like all of my other tries:

Hypothesis #3, Day 3

I walked up to a boy who was sitting in the grass near the fence at the edge of the park.

"Hiya!" I said with a little wave of my hand. *Ugh!* I thought to myself. *Who says* "hiya"? *What am I*

doing? I'm gonna blow it again!!

The boy was just sitting there, staring at me with a blank expression, just like all the other kids had done. *Oh no*, I thought, *here we go again*. BUT, just then, something incredible happened.

He said, "Hey, man, don't think I'm being rude, but I can't talk right now. I'm concentrating."

"Um, OK, sure. I get it." But I didn't *really* get it. I didn't get it at all. I had no idea what this was supposed to mean or what I was supposed to do next.

I was SO thankful when the boy spoke up again and said, "I

have to be completely still so she will get bored and fly away without stinging me." His eyes rolled up and to the left, bringing my attention to something crawling around the top of his hair.

I moved over a little closer to see what it was, and you'll never believe what I saw! It was a BEE!

Was this a sign? Was the universe telling me that this was my chance? Was this dude who was stuck like a statue supposed to be my new bro? I couldn't waste any more time thinking about it. I had to act … FAST!

Should I run away and save myself? *No! Bros stick together,* I told myself. I looked all around me for a weapon to rescue my new potential bro from a painful sting.

Should I hit him on the head with a stick? *No, probably not.* Should I trap the bee by dropping a big blob of mud on this guy's head? *That may be a bad idea too.* What

then? What should I use?

Just then, I noticed a patch of tall wildflowers peeking through the fence boards. I ran over and picked the tallest one I could find. I pointed the wildflower toward the bee like a knight pointing his joust at a fearsome dragon. The bee immediately jumped aboard my flower-joust, and I was able to carry it away and toss it into the woods.

"WOW—you handled that like a ninja!" he said. "Whew! Thank you so much. I have been sitting here with that bee on my head forever!"

"My name is Carlos. Oh, I almost forgot. Did you want to ask me something? What were you doing over here?"

"Oh, nothing," I said. "I was just looking for bees." I smiled and could feel my face returning to its normal face color and nonexploding face temperature.

After that, talking with Carlos was just ... easy! We actually don't have all that much in common, but

we had a few laughs over hearing what different weird things each of us is into.

For example, Carlos is a tri-county junior composition champion. (I had to ask what that means. He says it's a contest for music composers.) He uses his computer to actually make up music out of thin air! And he must make pretty good music if he is the champion! Mega-interesting!

While we were talking, another kid rode up on his bike.

"Hey, Carlos!" he shouted.

"Hey, what's up? Woodrow, this is Max. He just saved me from a killer bee!"

"Nice!" replied Woodrow. "Hey, I recognize you."

Oh no. Here it comes. I just knew he was going to say, "You're that weird boy who was freaking kids out at the park yesterday," but instead, he said, "Yeah, I know you. You're Miguel's friend, right?"

"Oh, yes, that's right. Miguel is my BEST friend, but did you hear he moved?"

"Yeah, total bummer, man. So, you're going into fifth, right? Who's

your teacher?"

"Yep, I'll be in fifth grade; Mrs. Hammersmith's class."

"Me too! Is it true that her nickname is Mrs. Hammerhead because she is deadly serious about talking in class?

I heard that one kid who was talking during math had to stay after school with her. No one ever saw him again. Some people think that he moved, but I don't know, man. I don't know ..."

MRS. HAMMERHEAD

"Ha ha. No, don't worry," I said. "My brother, Matt, had her. He said that she gave herself that nickname because she is a huge shark 'aficionado.' That means someone who really likes something and is an expert on it."

Uh-oh. I thought. *Was I being too much of a know-it-all?*

"Cool. Cool," said Woodrow. "You're kinda brainy, man. I dig it!" Woodrow had a weirdly cool way of saying things. He continued. "Well, anyway, I'm stoked that I have a friend in old Hammerhead's class."

All three of us laughed.

Did he just call me a FRIEND?

I thought, trying not to let them see my mega-excitement. *YESSSSSSS! The experiment worked, FINALLY!*

The three of us hung out for a while and then decided to meet back tomorrow at Carlos's house for a Spud tournament. There will be another kid there who's supposed to be unbeatable.

CHAPTER 12:
Conclusion

Fast-forward a couple of weeks, and now I am the proud owner of three new friends! Miguel (my classic bro) couldn't believe it when I told him, but he was really happy for me.

I GET my new bros,
    and my new bros GET me,
and, oh, by the way,
    one new bro is a SHE!

WOODROW

CARLOS

CAMI
(THE SPUD
CHAMP)

I have found where I fit
    in this cool little pack
of great kids who dig me and
        TOTES 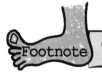 have my back!

OK, SO MAYBE THE
REAL ME ACTUALLY
TOTES LIKES ABBREVS...

Footnote | Totes = An abbrev for "totally."

92

FRIENDSHIP EXPERIMENT: CONCLUSION!

Now on to the scientific stuff: the results of my experiment. As for my hypothesis, the winning idea was to put myself out there, be myself, and most of all, keep trying!

I definitely learned a ton from all of my miserable failures. Here's the deal: yeah, it was so painfully awful at the time, but now when I think back to how nervous I was or how silly I must have looked in Matt's shirt, I just LAUGH! I

gotta tell ya—laughing about it feels a lot better than crying!

I learned something really important from my success too. Just because I don't fit IN doesn't mean that I don't fit *somewhere*. I want to fit with all the other people like me, who like to do their own thing, even if that makes them different. I think I will call this ...

FITTING OUT!

My new band of buddies,
    my posse, my tribe,
are others like me,
    who ROCK their own vibe.

We get along great,
    but each has their own quirks.
I'm not sure quite how,
    but just trust me, it works!

Each of us is different,
    I'm happy to say.
My new friends are WEiRD
    in the very best way.

So that's the conclusion of my friendship experiment. My advice to you is do *your* thing! If you haven't found *your* bees yet, keep looking. Don't give up! They are buzzing around you all the time; you probably just don't realize it.

And I'm still the same guy
that I've always been.
From now on, I'd rather
fit OUT than fit IN!

GLOSSARY

(The words are in the same order that you see them in the book.)

Tardigrade (water bear) – An eight-legged micro-animal with a segmented body that lives in water and can survive in a variety of harsh conditions that other animals cannot.

Bio – Short for "biography," which is the story or study of a person.

Yurt – A circular tent structure first used centuries ago by nomads in Central Asia. Today the term also includes modern one-room homes.

Bouillabaisse – A traditional seafood stew that originated in Marseille, a city on the coast of France.

Aerodynamics – The study of how objects move through the air and how air moves around objects.

"Drag" is a type of aerodynamic force that occurs when air moves in the opposite direction of a moving object, having the effect of slowing it down. *Think of a parachute: the fabric is used to create drag force and slow the speed of a falling object.*

Scientific method – a process used to

explain how or why things happen in our world. The process is made up of different steps related to asking questions, experimenting, seeing what happens, and then figuring out what it all means.

Hypothesis – An idea you can prove (or disprove) by testing it.

Tai Chi – A form of martial arts, originating in China, that is made up of slow, controlled movements and balance exercises.

Geocaching – An outdoor treasure hunt where participants follow clues and/or coordinates, often with the help of GPS, to find a special item left by previous 'cachers.

Adios – A Spanish-language word for "goodbye."

Caper – A wild and exciting adventure to get, sometimes even steal, something of great value. (No stealing in my experiment though!)

Jinx – A game played when two people accidentally say the same word at the same time. One player can act fast and count to ten, declaring that the other player either has to buy them something (classically a soda) or wait until the winner says their name before they are allowed to speak again.

Posse – A group of people who join together for a common purpose or goal.

Quirk – An unusual behavior or part of someone's personality that makes them unique.

SPUD – Game Rules and How to Play

First, you need a soft ball. I mean, a REALLY soft ball. So soft that if it hit you in the face, you would still be laughing. Surely you have heard the saying "There's no crying in SPUD." This is why.

Next, you need at least four players, but more is even better. The more players you have, the more fun it is.

To start, one person volunteers or is elected to be "IT." The other players each count off a number, 1, 2, 3, etc.

The person who is "IT" has the ball, and the other players stand around IT in a circle. IT throws the ball as high as he/she can and at the same time shouts out the number of one of the other players.

All of the players (including IT) run as far away from the center as possible EXCEPT for the player whose number was called. That player (2) runs to the center to try to catch the ball. As soon as she has the ball in her hands, she yells "SPUD," and all of the other players have to stop running.

Player 2 can now take three giant steps to get as close as possible to the player of her choice. Player 2 then has to throw the ball, trying to hit the other player. Player 3 can try to dodge the ball by leaning out of its way BUT cannot move his feet.

If player 2 hits the other player, then that player (3) gets an "S" and becomes IT. If player 2 misses, then player 2 gets an "S" and remains IT. The next time player 2 misses or gets hit by another IT, she will earn a "P," and then a "U," and so on.

Players continue to play rounds until a player earns "S-P-U-D," at which point, they are out of the game and have to sit out and watch. The last man (or woman) standing wins the game!

About the Author:

This is a photo of Sarah Giles when she was in third grade, making her favorite funny face. Why? Because it makes her laugh. Wearing a leotard instead of a shirt. Why? Because it's fun. And all the while, not caring a bit what anyone else might think about that.

She thinks of that time in her life as the golden age of joy, creativity, and fearless ME-dom.

BONUS: Confession of a stick figure girl.

You might remember me from the Friendship Experiment.

Then again, you might NOT remember me. That is the way it used to go for me.

Most times, people didn't really notice that I was there. Even if they did notice, they quickly forgot about me. I blended in so well, you could hardly tell if I was standing right next to you.

What's worse is that the kids at school sometimes called me "Chameleon" because I sort of "disappeared" into the background, and also because of my name.

I was so excited one day when a new boy who I had never seen at the park before came up to ME! I thought maybe he would even talk to me. He seemed really nice, but he didn't ever say anything.

I have thought about this moment

over and over since it happened. Someone finally noticed me and was about to talk to me, and I blew it!

Why didn't I say anything? If I had just said something ... anything, maybe I could have made a new friend.

He seemed really upset that I didn't say hello. He even ran away ... literally! Didn't he realize that I was not used to anyone noticing me, especially talking to me?

Surely he just lost interest in me and decided to leave. I wish I could be better at speaking up ...

UPDATE: In the last month of summer vacation, I grew three whole inches! I am now the second tallest kid in the whole fifth grade. I am literally head and shoulders above almost everyone around me. I'm even taller than my mom!

I am so tall that I am now often the *first* one people notice, instead of the last! (I also dyed my hair purple and wear brightly colored clothes, just in case I am sitting down and people don't realize how tall I am.)

Oh, how great it feels to not be invisible anymore! Now that people can see me, I am getting more used to talking too. I guess I was never really afraid to speak up, I just didn't have that much practice talking to people. It is a nice feeling to have someone interested to hear what I have to say, for a change!

And that boy from the park? I DID see him again. And we even had the chance to become good friends. He calls me one of his "bros." I don't mind, because I know that it means something good.

Also, no one calls me Chameleon anymore, they just call me by name:

Camille Lianne. You can just call me Cami.

Read more of Cami's story at the end of FITTING OUT Book #2: The Cool Kid Paradox!

Books in the FiTTiNG OUT series

1. The Friendship Experiment

2. The Cool Kid Paradox

3. The Nitpicker's Dilemma

Switches and Peeps have their own books too!

Perfect for readers ages 6-8.

Made in the USA
Middletown, DE
14 December 2022

18636911R00076